Dust Under My Feet

This little book is dedicated to my mother. She has been my inspiration and I have seen her working her way through so many tough times to make it to where she is now. If I ever felt like giving up she was always there to motivate me to carry on and to push me towards becoming a better and stronger person.

Dust Under My Feet

A Collection of Short Stories

Mahshid (Mushu) Khoshbakht

To order additional copies of this book, contact:
Xlibris Corporation
1-888-795-4274
www.Xlibris.com
Orders@Xlibris.com
38937

CONTENTS

Happily Ever After 7

Tick Tock 14

Puzzle..18

8: 45...29

Today Is My Last Day 35

A Stranger's Smile..43

Dust Under My Feet 51

HAPPILY EVER AFTER

Sarah looked up from her keyboard and stared at the empty word document on her screen. After working for an hour on her paper she had yet to write a passable sentence.

Sarah was a thin pale girl. Her hair was blonde and her eyes were blue. She was a German born American girl who had lived most of her 22 years in America. She never saw a reason to learn her native tongue. When she entered college she picked up a year of it and then dropped it the coming year.

William came up behind her and placed his hands on her shoulders. "Why don't you come to bed?" He leaned down and kissed her neck. "Finish it later." William was a bit chubbier than her. His skin was just as pale and his hair was just as golden. He had green eyes with a hint of hazel. She had met him in the second year of high school when she had been stuck with him as a lab partner the day her original partner caught a bad case of the flue. They had been together ever since.

The apartment was dark with only one lamp on the computer desk. "I don't have time later." She took her glasses off and leaned back against her chair letting her head hit his stomach. "I have classes all day tomorrow."

"What about the break in between? You don't have anything around lunch time."

"I have a lunch date with Alice."

"Cancel it." He rubbed her shoulders in an attempt to calm her down.

"I can't." Sarah persisted. "I already canceled on her God knows how many times before." She closed her eyes for a few seconds before opening them to look up at him.

William smiled down at her. "You look lovely."

"I look horrible Will. Don't even . . ." She shook her head and smiled back at him.

"I'm not. YOU look lovely."

She put her hand on his. "I need to get back to work." She sat up once again.

"Fine baby. Just try to finish and get some sleep." He kissed her neck one more time before walking back to the bedroom.

Sarah smiled to herself. "All right." Thirty more minuets passed and she finally had a few pages down. "I guess I just needed a little kiss." She stood up and walked to the fridge. As she placed a glass on the counter she heard a small clicking noise coming from the door. The house was so quiet that even a little noise was easily detectable. She glanced over at the door. "How many times do I have to tell him to lock the door?" She closed the fridge while talking to herself and walked past the counter.

As she reached for the lock the door suddenly flung open and she was knocked on to the floor. In front of her stood a man dressed all in black. His face was hidden in the darkness. All she could see was the shine of a barrel of his gun.

"Sarah? Are you okay?" William stopped dead in his tracks and then exited the bedroom.

She couldn't speak or move an inch.

"Ey man!" the stranger pointed the gun to her. "Stay back!"

"I'm not moving." William tried to stay calm as he put his hands up. "What do you want?"

"Whatever you got!" He threw a bag at him. Sarah felt a tight grip on her arm as he yanked her up and placed the gun at her head. "Move." He pushed her ahead. "Put whatever you have in there." He spoke to William. "Don't do anything stupid. I know how to use this." At this point Sarah couldn't help but to start crying.

"It's in the bedroom."

"Then go get it!"

William walked into the bedroom slowly.

"You do anything stupid and she is f**king dead!" The man yelled back at him.

"Will . . ." Sarah managed to get her voice out. A few seconds later, William was back with a bag full of their money and jewels. "Take it." He held it out. "Take it and get out."

The man reached his free hand out to get the bag. A blade of a knife met his hand. William grabbed his other arm as fast as he could to prevent a misfire. The man pulled his hand away and stepped back the gun still in his hand. It was all in a blink of an eye. One gunshot went off and the man was gone.

Williams face and shirt where covered in blood. Sarah's body laid in front of his feet.

"No . . . No. No!" He got down on the floor and turned her over in his arms. His voice was shaky and his face soaked with bloody tears "Sarah?! Baby! Come on. Look at me!" Nothing changed.

*   *   *

A few days had past since the incident. "Anything?" William was sitting outside a hospital room.

"She is awake." A man in a white lab coat was standing in front of him as he spoke. "But it seems although the bullet missed anything that would be fatal or damaging she doesn't seem to be able to remember anything. It's like it was all too much of a shock to her"

"What the hell do you mean?" William stood up and turned to go into the room.

"Sir please you cannot go in there now." The man stopped him at the door.

"The hell I can't go in there!" He pushed the doctor away and opened the door. The anger on his face disappeared as he gazed at her bed.

Sarah was sitting up. She wore nothing but a hospital gown. Her hair was gone and now some white bandages covered her head. A nurse was sitting across from her holding up a spoon to her. She glanced at William for a moment before coming back to Sarah. "Okay honey. Can you tell me what this is?"

Sarah just stared at it.

"Can you hold this for me?" She grabbed her hand and put it around the spoon. Sarah grasped the spoon with both hands before dropping it. The nurse picked it up once again. "Spoon." She held it up to her.

Sarah opened her mouth but closed it before any words came out.

The nurse put her hand down and smiled at her. "Okay sweetie. You did good." She slowly pushed her back down. "Get some rest." She looked up at William and started walking towards him.

"Oh God . . . !" Williams covered his face with his hand as he started weeping. He shook his head and fell against the doorway.

"Come on sweetie. She needs her rest. Let's get you some water." The elderly nurse slowly guided him out of the room.

"How could this happen?" William sat in the white plastic chair across from the nurse. He sipped some water from the white cup. "The doctor said when she wakes up she should be fine. He said she was lucky." He tried to hold the tears back.

"Just give it time honey." The nurse patted him on the shoulder before walking away.

"Give it time . . . F**k!" He threw the cup against the wall and pushed his chair back before exiting the cafeteria and leaving the hospital.

*   *   *

It was two months later. Sarah was still at the hospital. She had learned to eat by herself now and could do almost everything alone.

"Hey baby." William walked up to her and gave her a flower. Her hair had grown quite a bit now and she had started to remember her life. She remembered William and many memories with him. "Are you feeling well today?" He kissed her forehead and smiled.

She smiled and pointed to a chair next to her. She still couldn't fully talk and had been writing down everything she wanted to say.

"I'm sorry I wasn't here after class yesterday. I had a test I really needed to take." He sat down on the chair. William had devoted his time to helping her. He took a night job and would come everyday at 10 AM when she woke up. He would stay with her for five hours before going to class and then coming back after three hours. He would nap with her when she took her naps and then stay with her till she went to sleep around 9 PM before he went back to work.

She picked up the paper and wrote 'It's all right. I understand. Did you do well?"

"Of course. Oh! Look!" He started moving his hands. Sarah had started learning sign language to help her communicate.

"Was that right?" William asked. "I want to take you to dinner. Right?" She smiled and clapped for him.

"Here." He placed a bag on her bed. "I will go get ready. I got this for you."

"Hello sweetie" The nurse came in. During her time in the hospital Janice had been helping Sarah. Ever since she first tried to teach her what a spoon was she had grown to love Sarah like a daughter.

"Hey Janice. Sarah she will help you get ready. I'll see you tonight." He smiled and kissed her once before leaving the room.

"Oh my god! It's beautiful. Where did you get it?" Janice picked the dress up and looked at it. Sarah smiled and pointed at the door. "Oh a date?! Wow! Lucky man! Come on come on! Let's dress you up."

That night he took her to a beautiful place. They had a table on the roof. There was no one else there due to him reserving the whole place so they could be alone. The dinner passed and so did the desert. Both had been pre-made and set up for them. "Sarah. Can I ask you something?"

She nodded and looked at his hands as they spoke out a sentence. She looked at him confused.

"It wasn't right? I think it's right."

Sarah grabbed his arm to stop him from rambling. "Marry?"

"What? What? Did you just . . . ?" William's smile got bigger than ever. "You spoke."

"Will . . . William." Her words didn't sound quite right, like a deaf person learning to talk, but to William's ears this was an angel singing.

"Yes. Yes!" He got out of his chair and on one knee. "I should do it right. Will you . . ." He took a box out of his pocket. "Marry me?" He looked up at her as he opened the box and revealed to her the most beautiful ring. Sarah started to cry more than she had even that night. "Yes!" She signed out as she spoke. "Yes!" Williams put the box down and stood up. "I Love you." Sarah said as she stood up and jumped onto him almost causing him to fall.

"I love you too. God! I'm the luckiest person alive!"

Sarah stood back a bit and kissed him. "No one can live in denial forever." Her speech was almost normal this time. "You think I didn't know?"

William smiled at her.

"Every time I would tell Janice you visited me she would just look at me and smile or she would just nod."

"It was a week after. I couldn't handle it." William took a few steps back. He turned around and walked over to the ledge. "I wasn't strong. I wasn't as strong as you, but I couldn't just leave you because of my own stupid mistake. After I jumped I still couldn't leave. I didn't want to." He turned around and looked at her. Her black dress was loose and following in the rooftop breeze as did his coat.

She stepped forward and took his hand. "I know. I don't blame you. I never did William." She kissed his cheek. "I'm engaged to a ghost and I couldn't be happier." Her eyes where shining with tears as she looked at him. "Let's get married when we meet again. Okay?" She moved one leg off the ledge and with those last few words she flew towards the ground and William followed. As her body hit the pavement, his disappeared into the ground and this was their "happily ever after."

TICK TOCK

The hand is moving so slowly. I am sitting there staring at it. You think I'm exaggerating, don't you? You aren't here. It is driving me insane. I feel like I am stuck in one of those things. What were they called? Oh yea, "ant farm". I feel stuck in there. I can't get out. Do I want to?

I don't know anymore. I feel like doing it. But it doesn't feel right. Was it my fault? No! No! It couldn't be. I didn't do anything, right?

I shouldn't be here. I keep thinking it over and over again, saying it to myself. "You didn't do it Mark! You didn't do anything." How many times have I said that? Oh yea, twenty-eight.

I'm counting. It's my entertainment in this little "ant farm". What else am I supposed to do? Bite my tongue repeatedly like a nervous moron?

I won't lie. I considered it. I didn't do it though. That would make this worse.

What am I doing here? Why am I sitting here? I shouldn't be in here! I shouldn't! Let me out!

I want to scream this out loud, right now, but I can't. I'll just scream it in my head. It's satisfying as it is.

I know they are looking at me. I can sense these things. Most people can. You feel eyes on you. You can feel it when people are talking about you only a few feet away even if you cannot hear their babbling nonsensical voices.

I know they are examining me, even though this glass window separates us. I can't see the other side. They think I'm stupid. They're taunting me. I'm not an idiot. I know you are watching me.

I'm not going to talk. I will sit here and watch that clock.

Tick Tock . . .

Why a metal table? It's cold. This chair isn't making it any better on me right now.

Maybe I'll just fiddle my thumbs on the table.

No! No!

Stop it!

They notice.

Stop it!

It's making you look bad Mark! Stop!

All right, just keep my hands there. Steady as a rock. Am I steady? Am I?

I think I'm shaking! No. It's just your imagination Mark. You're thinking too much.

Tick Tock . . .

I can hear myself breath in here.

In

Out

In

Out

It's loud. What if they can hear it? They can hear it! They think I'm nervous! I'm not!

I have no reason to be. I don't belong here.

When he was in here, he was talking to me like I was one of *them*. He thought I was one of *them*! Fool. I'm not.

He looked at me like I was lower than him. His voice was cold. He didn't care. I saw him fiddling with his tie. He was tired.

He doesn't care! He wants to finish this and go home! Maybe to his wife, maybe he has kids.

"Did you do it? Just give me a yes or no answer!"

He yelled that at me, four times. I counted again.

"No!"

I said that, four times.

He won't believe me. Why won't he believe me? Mark Why won't he believe you?

Maybe he is right Mark. Maybe you do belong in here. Maybe you are one of *them*.

Shut up!

Mark! You're not! This is what they have been trying to do!

Stop fiddling with your thumbs. You're doing it again. Stop.

It's choppier. The breathing is getting less steady. I can hear it.

They have nothing on you! Steady. There Mark. That's better. Calm.

The water is shaking. It's just in the glass. Why is it shaking? There is no wind. My leg! Mark! Stop tapping your foot on the ground. Mark! Stop it. The whole table is shaking Mark. They will notice. They will hear! Why is it so loud! Stop the tapping! It's like a drum! Stop Mark.

Tick Tock . . .

Click,

The door is opening. Don't look up. Stare at your hands. No! No! Look up Mark. Look up at him. He is still wearing his badge but the suit jacket is gone. His tie is ruffled. He has been messing with it. He just wants to go. He probably doesn't even care about you Mark! No one cares. They don't think you are a human being. They think you are one of *them*!

"Get up!"

Follow what he says.

A drop of water on the floor? How did that get there? Wait. Why is he looking at me?

"I left you alone in here for five minutes and you are sweating this much? Didn't think it was so hot in here . . ." He looks doubtful again! Do something!

I'm just smiling at him. "Overactive sweat glands, what can you do?" He is undoing the handcuffs.

"I hear ya."

Follow him out the door Mark.

"Sorry for the misunderstanding. You are no longer a suspect in the murder of Alexander Gonzales and his sister. Need a ride?" He is waiting for an answer, looking at you. Don't look at his eyes Mark! Shake your head.

Good. Good. Leave.

Tick Tock . . .

A restroom in a gas station,

What?! Why!? Why is it still there! They didn't see it? How!? How did they not see all this red! Maybe it's the mirror.

No! It's clean! Nothing there! Wash it off! Faster! Faster! Use more soup! Use more. Get rid of the shirt! Throw it away.

There. A trash can.

Wash it! More soup! It won't come off. I'm shaking, sweating, tears. I feel *them* Mark! You are being weak!

"Sir?" Freeze. I see his reflection. Must work at the gas station.

"Are you all right sir?"

"Don't you see it!?" He is looking frightened when I'm clinging to his shoulders. He is afraid Mark! He is afraid of you. "Don't you see all this blood!? It won't come off! It won't come off!" I taste my own blood in my mouth. My teeth hurt. Mark you idiot! You are grinding them so hard!

"What blood? Sir . . . There is nothing on you but water and soup."

PUZZLE

This is how it all started

    The murmurs of the town were more than enough to make anyone wonder. Everyone has heard it. *I'm crazy*, they say. No one believed me then. No one believes me now. I suppose it's for the best. Maybe if they knew, they would be crazy too. Sometimes I think to myself: "Hey! . . . Don't you want them to suffer too? Do you hear the sh*t they say about you?" I ignore all that. What's the point anyways? Right? I live with this burden. I don't want to share it with anyone else. You would be like me too if you had seen the things I've seen. Picture it in your head.

Picture the one you love.

Your wife,

Your best friend,

Your son,

Your daughter,

Your mother,

Your father,

Maybe it's even your pet.

Do you have that pictured in your head? Now see them through my eyes, limb by limb, being ripped apart.

Are you crazy too now?

Are you like me now?

This is what I did

"Detective!" The lady dressed in a summer dress sat across the clustered table. Her purse was nicely placed on her lap where her hands laid over it.

"Sir?" She said again a bit more loudly. "Detective Chen?"

"Yes?" He stared at her.

What a weird guy. If he was listening why didn't he just answer me sooner? She thought to herself.

"I was told to come here by that gentleman over there . . ." She tilted her head a bit to show who she had just mentioned.

Detective Chen cleaned some papers off the desk and placed them on the floor. "Here!" He took out a piece of paper and placed a pencil on it. "Write your name and phone number on this." He slid it with one hand across the desk.

She did as she was told and slid the paper and pencil back towards him.

"Go." The man stood up and walked away from the desk.

"How rude . . . !" She said under her breath and put her bag over her shoulder and walked out of the building guided by a female security guard.

Detective Chen dropped the paper on the desk of a colleague, a new detective who until a week a go had been working under Chen himself. The name on his desk read Edward Lee.

"What's this?" Lee said as he placed his coffee cup down on the table. His eyes were still glowed to his computer screen.

"Her info." Chen answered.

"Ah. Thank Ya." He stopped as he looked at the paper. "There is nothing here but a name and a number. You were supposed to interview her about what she saw." Lee picked the paper up and turned his chair to face Chen. "Not my job." Chen walked over to the coffee pot on the table in the corner of the huge room, which was over-crowded by desks, very messy ones.

Lee rubbed his eyes in frustration and jammed the paper into his pants pocket. His gaze turned back to the computer screen.

"You sure have been acting like an ass today dad." A much younger man walked up to him and started pouring himself some coffee.

"We are at work. Use the proper title." Detective Chen poured some cream into his coffee.

"All right then Alex."

"Detective Chen."

"Detective Chen. You sure have been acting like an ass today."

Alex ignored the comment and walked back to his desk with the coffee.

"Get back to work Mike. Stop harassing Detective Chen" A higher up ordered Alex's son who took the order with a smile and proceeded to doing his own work.

"We got another call!" Someone yelled across the room.

"Let's go." Alex said as he put on his coat and walked out the door. Edward soon followed behind him walking as he fastened his gun into place.

"Where is it this time?" Alex opened the car door and sat in.

"Kideona Park." Edward said as Alex started the car and started driving.

"What do we know?"

"It's the same as before, exact copy down to the last cut. This killer must be one damn sad guy with too much time on his hand."

"Aren't they all?" Alex said as he drove with one hand.

Edward laughed slightly. "More pathetic than the rest. Every single cut is so precise."

"Skin gone again?"

"Yea. This time it's the right cheek. Sick bastard. Why would you take that? Souvenir from a kill?"

"A human puzzle . . ." Alex said to himself.

"What?"

"Nothing. Get out. We are here." He got out of the car and closed the door shut.

The area was closed off by rows of yellow keep-out tapes. Many people crowded around it. Some even were taking pictures with their cell phones. A few police officers gathered around the body, which was tied to a pole with a rope. A few knives placed neatly as if they were safety pins used to keep something in place. The victim was a female.

Alex stepped over the tape followed by Edward.

"Detective, you are fast." A man in his 40s, maybe a few years younger than Alex approached the two.

"Who do we have this time?" Alex asked as he put on some gloves and started taking the knives off and placing them into evidence bags and handing them to Edward.

"Sarah Marshal, twenty four years old. She was probably on a walk in the park at night, perhaps walking her dog."

"How do we know this?" Edward asked as he examined the body.

"She had her ID in her pocket." He handed the plastic bag, which held the bloody ID to Alex.

"And once again . . ." The man pointed to the girl's cheek. "Some skin is gone. It's like he is collecting different skin types."

"If you want to meet weird people, our job is the best." Edward added.

"Take the body down. Send the rope to the evidence room and send the body in for an autopsy." Alex walked away as he took his phone out. "I need to make a call." He stated. He looked around as he waited for the phone to be answered.

"Hello! Chen residence, Millie speaking." A childish female voice answered. "Hey! Is mom there?" Alex replied.

"Daddy! Yea! Are you coming over for dinner tonight?" She asked.

"Yes. Put your mother on the phone."

A few seconds passed and then a new voice came from the phone. "Hello Alex." Her voice was soft and sounded kind.

"Hey. Vic is going to eat dinner with you guys tonight. I'm afraid I can't make it. I have work to do."

"Vic called and said he can't make it tonight already."

"What?"

"He said he was going over to a friend. Needed to work on a case with him."

"All right. I will talk to you later."

"Take care Alex. You work too much." His ex-wife said caringly.

"I will. Tell Millie I said I love her." He sighed. "Have to go back to work now. Goodbye." He flung his cell shut and walked to the car, in which Edward was already sitting.

"Talking to the ex-wife again?" He asked.

Alex nodded and started driving back to the station. "Don't ever get married. It's too much trouble."

"Is it? Maybe you're just bad at it." Edwards rolled the window down and placed his arm out the window. "Is she Chinese too?" He asked Alex. "I would guess so since Victor is."

"Stop talking to me" Alex never liked talking about personal things at work. No matter how close he was with someone. He barely even talked to his own son.

Edward placed his arm on the windowsill of the car and closed his eyes. "I don't think I am getting any sleep tonight."

The rest of the car ride was quiet with only the sound of the cars passing by and wind.

This is how it ends. No regrets.

The office was quiet on that day. No one wanted to talk. It's been three months since that case started. It wasn't over yet. Everyone was so tired of it. They all wanted to give up. It wasn't going to stop until they caught him though. They couldn't stop now. They almost had it.

It was a quiet day. It had been a quiet week. It happened in the beginning of the week. The bodies where showing up in the park and around it since Sarah's was found. The smart thing was to stay there over night and watch out for him. Maybe he would show up.

Edward had volunteered to go. Alex being his partner was obviously the choice to go with him. There was one problem. He was sick, just a mild cold. But for a man his age that little cold was hard to bear at times.

"I'll go instead of my father—Detective Chen." Mike had said on that day. Alex objected. They had sent him home to rest that day. No one wanted their top detective to be sick.

He hated his son for taking his place that day till this day.

They sat in the car for three hours. That's how the story was told by Edward.

"I went out to get some air. I wanted to have a look around." Edward explained the night before. "He had his gun on him." He had objected when detective Alex had yelled at him for leaving Mike alone in the car.

"I was gone for maybe five minuets." His face and voice held sadness in them as he spoke. "I didn't hear anything. You said it. There was no struggling. He was knocked out with some sort of . . . something. The handkerchief trick, maybe some kind of chemical." He continued. "I came back. It was dark so it looked normal to me at first, . . . then . . ." This is where Alex had walked out. The remaining people walked him. He had grabbed his coat and went out. He said he went to get some coffee. No one blamed him. It would be hard for anyone to hear this, being told about their own son.

A few seconds of silence passed. Edward kept his gaze on the middle table. ". . . then I looked closer." He continued. His voice was soft. "I . . . My hand was on his seat. I felt the blood on my hand. That's when I called. I checked on him. I tried to wake him up." His hand was in his hair covering one of his eyes with the palm.

"That's how you got the blood on you." One of the interviewers had said to him.

"That's how I got his. Um. His blood." Edward let out a small sigh. "That's how I got his blood on me." He nodded slowly.

They had let him go after that. He came back to work two days later.

Mike's body was examined. Alex was in the room with them. He saw his son's lifeless face. He saw it with his own eyes. He was the one that discovered the patch of skin missing from the back of his thigh. After pointing it out, he ground his teeth together and looked away. They could see the tears in his eyes.

People knew how he felt. Alex himself tried to hide it even though he knew that the others could see it on his face. He looked older since that day. There seemed to be more wrinkles on his face, more pain in his movements.

"Take a week off." Edward sat down in one of the visitor's chairs that were lined up on the wall. He faced Alex as he spoke to him.

Alex looked up from his papers for only one second before going back to work.

"I took some time off . . . Why don't you? You need it Alex. Have you seen yourself in the mirror lately?"

He was completely ignored this time.

Edward sighed and stood up.

"Sir! You have one smart son. Even when he is dead." A fellow worker walked up next to Alex's desk where he was sitting. "He thought of it all." He placed a plastic bag over Alex's papers.

"My son's hair?" Alex put his pen down and leaned back in his chair as Edward joined the two.

"Ah. No sir. This is the hair we found in your sons pocket. Remember?"

"Yeah." Edward picked the bag up and looked at it. "It wasn't his? I figured it was pulled out and fell in there when he was struggling." He said.

Alex grabbed the bag from him. "This is . . ." He stood up. "Did you get it tested?" He yelled. The whole room now had his attention.

"Yes sir. This is the killer's hair. The results are being faxed over as we speak." The man answered with a smile.

"Jesus. It's finally over!" A fellow worker yelled out.

Everyone in the room seemed so much livelier now.

"All right then! Good few months of work everyone!" Edward added with a laugh that was followed by a few more people. "I'm going to go get us some celebratory cake!" He grabbed his keys and headed out the door with a big smile on his face.

"Hey! It's not done, . . . Yet" Even Alex was smiling as he spoke. "Ah. He has done much work. I'll let him off this time."

"The fax is here." Alex and a few others gathered around the fax machine waiting for the paper to print out the face of their killer.

It seemed like they had been working on this for years. Many lives had been lost. Many hurt.

"You did great . . . Son. You did great." Alex said so calmly, a warm look graced his face. A few hands patted him on the shoulder. The room was silent then.

"I guess they were right. Sometimes the enemy is closer than you think."

Alex's eyes widened as he ran out the door followed by a few more people and the peaceful atmosphere of the office was suddenly gone. People were on the phones and running out the door as if the end of the world has come.

Alex yelled out orders as he got in his car.

Everyone obeyed and went to their destinations.

The police siren on his car was now turned on as he speeded through the streets.

"Come on! Come on!" His cell was to his face.

"No answer?" The man next to him said.

"Sh*t!" Alex slammed the phone to the window.

"Go! Go!" He yelled to the cars and dashed past them.

Only a few minutes later they arrived at their destination. A few other police cars parked next to him. "All right. You two go through the back. We'll meet you at the door. Stay in the back. I'll go up with Clark through the front." Alex gave his orders as everyone got their guns out and got ready. "You two!" He pointed. "Go stand at the back door and be ready. Go!" He and Clark ran into the building and up the stairs.

They were now at the door and against the wall. The others soon came running the other way and lined up, as did Alex and Clark on the other wall.

"Come out now." Alex said. His voice seemed calm. "Just come out. Don't make this harder than it has to be."

No answer came.

"We're going in." Alex whispered. He reached for the doorknob. ". . . . Open?" He twisted it and opened the door. The room was dark.

"I waited for so long." The voice came from the dark room. Alex pointed his gun toward the couch.

"Why did you do this?" He asked.

"Ah!" Clark said as he looked away from the wall, which his gaze was up on. He looked like as he was about to throw up his lunch. "Detective!" He pointed at the wall with a free hand.

Alex looked over.

"What the hell is this!?"

On the wall was an outline off a human body. "The skin, . . . You took." The skin patched missing from the victim's bodies was placed on the inside of the outline. Each piece put neatly in place where it should be on the outline.

"I just wanted to finish my puzzle." The voice said.

"You . . . Sick F**ker!" Alex dropped his gun and ran towards the man. The man didn't resist. He let himself be handcuffed and dragged out of the room.

"You murdered so many people! So many. You killed my son! You! You killed Mike!" Alex had him pinned against the wall and was now punching him.

"Sir! Detective Chen!" Clark grabbed Alex and pulled him away. "Calm down!" After a few others had hold of the detective, Clark proceeded toward the man who still had a sick smile on his face.

"You are still smiling . . . You're just sick . . . You killed all those people . . . Still don't have a reason?" Clark pinned the man to the wall face forward and then yanked him back and started guiding him out.

"I gave you one. I just wanted . . ." He smiled at Clark. "To-Finish-My-Puzzle."

"Shut up!" There were now out and forcing him into the car as many people watched and took pictures. The police cars made a disco field of the place as they shined in the night.

"You are under arrest for the murder of many innocent people, Edward Lee." He closed the door behind him and got in the passenger seat of Alex's car. Alex was sitting in there watching the car containing the killer driving away.

"I wouldn't have thought. Really" Clark sighed. "I'm just glad it's over."

"Still has a smile on his face . . . Even now that he is driving away to his death."

"I think he knew it all along. It seemed like he wanted to get caught." Clark looked at Alex. "Did you see it? There was a piece of his . . . human puzzle missing, on the chest."

Alex thought for a moment then nodded. "Over the heart."

Clark finished the detective's thoughts for him. "It wouldn't have mattered if we caught him or not. He would be dead either way. That sick bastard was going to cut out his own heart to finish . . . His puzzle."

And this was how it ends. No regrets.

Sincerely Yours,

Edward Lee

8: 45

The Time After

"I'm sorry. There is nothing else we can do."

Those were the last words Alex Parker heard. He had always heard these words on TV as he had flipped through the drama-filled shows but he never thought he would hear them being said about him as he lies in a hospital bed.

"There has to be something else you can do." His wife's voice rang through the room "He can't just be stuck like this!" She yelled at the doctor standing next to Alex's bed.

"Mrs. Parker. We did all we could. I'm sorry. The rest is up to you." He rubbed his eyes with one hand as he looked down at the clipboard in his hand. He looked back up at her. "These machines will keep him alive."

She cut him off "You call this alive?" She sat down on the chair next to his bed and grabbed Alex's hand.

"I don't." Dr. Keen looked over at her with a saddened look in his eyes. "It's not my place to make this decision, but please listen to me. There is nothing else we can do to help your husband except make him as comfortable as we can." He walked over to the front of the bed as he spoke. The doctor placed the clipboard back in the holder. "It's your choice to decide to pull the plug or not. Keep this in mind."

She looked over at his direction as she wiped her tears away with a handkerchief.

"In this hospital alone there are dozens of people waiting for an organ just so they can live normally." He gave her a small smile and walked out closing the door.

Sarah Parker stared at her husband lying in bed with machine tubes attached to him like he was a robot in the making. She sat there by his bedside and cried for the next hour.

"Mom." The door opened slowly as her son, Josh, walked in. "It's late. We should head home." He was a young boy who was just finishing his last year of high school. He walked over to the bed and helped his mother up. "We'll come back tomorrow." He looked over at his father. He was a fit man, only 45 years old. This was not a man someone would expect to see in such a place. Josh had his father's features. The strong jaw and jet black hair. His eyes were the hazel color of his mother's. His younger sister had gotten the mother's blonde hair. "Cindy called. Jenny is finally asleep." He broke his gaze from his father and back onto his mother. "We need to head back. You know she is going to wake up in the middle of the night and start crying. Cindy has done enough babysitting for this night."

Sarah looked over at her husband one last time before handing the car keys to Josh and walking out of the hospital with him.

The drive home was silent. It was just the end of winter and the weather was dry and cold. The rain was pouring down that night as it had the night his father had gone out to buy some milk for the next morning's breakfast.

They arrived at home an hour later. Josh took one last look at the car clock before turning the car off. The time read 1: 36 AM. He walked over to the other side of the car with the umbrella and walked his mother to the door. They were greeted by Cindy who smiled and gave Sarah a hug before leaving.

Josh sat on the couch and waited for his mother to take a warm shower. He leaned forward in his sit and rested his face in his hands with a loud sigh. He thought about what had happened. It had been three months but he still remembered clearly. His father had left to go buy some milk as a request from his mother. The rain was heavy and the roads were slick. It hadn't taken much for him to loose control of his wheel. They had spent four hours in the hospital doing the best they could but in the end his father had lost all connections to his brain.

"What would you do?" Sarah spoke as she walked over and sat next to him.

"What?" Josh lifted his head up still leaning forward.

"Would you pull the plug?"

He looked away and let out another loud sigh. "Yes. Look around mother. He is not getting any better, but there are so many others that can. Don't you think it's selfish?"

"It might be, but he is my husband. He is your father! How could you even say that?" She shook her head and stood up to walk away.

"I would be proud of him."

"Proud of what? Him dying?" Sarah looked away trying to hold the tears back.

Josh stood up and walked past her to his room upstairs as he spoke. "No."

He stopped at the stairs for a moment before stepping up. "Of him saving lives."

The Days After

The next morning Josh and his mother went to the hospital. Dr. Keen greeted them and offered them some coffee, which only Josh took.

"How is he doing?" Josh asked. He took a sip of his coffee.

"I'm afraid it's still the same. Have you decided what you are going to do?"

Josh glanced over at his mother who was just sitting over by Alex's bed and holding his hand. She whispered to him as if her words would heal him.

"Stop it." He called out to her. "Just stop." He put the coffee down and walked out of the room.

Dr. Keen followed him out. "Listen." He stopped him and asked him to sit down.

"Your mother is having a hard time dealing with this. You have to try to understand. I know you're still young, but-"

"I'm 18. This kind of forces people to grow up."

Keen nodded. "You just have to understand what she is going through. They have been married for 20 years. Understand that." He patted him on the shoulder and walked back to join Sarah in the room.

Josh nodded to himself and stood up only to be shocked out of his mind by a loud entrance. He looked over at the door as it flew open. All he could hear were scattered words and yelling. Ten to fifteen gurneys flew past him. He couldn't count. Mothers, wives, husbands, fathers, and kids followed the crowd. Dr. Keen rushed out of the room and down the hall.

Josh ran into the room. "What happened?" He asked his mother who was standing at the door.

"I don't know. He said something about a bus accident. I don't know." She looked around confused. Josh could hear the lady over the intercom asking for doctors and surgeons; for nurses and others. He ran over through the bustling hospital and to the woman standing at the help desk.

"What's going on?"

"I'm sorry son I can not help-"

"I just asked what happened!"

"There was an accident. Please back away and get out of the way." She sounded annoyed as she spoke.

He took the hint and backed away.

He could see doctors running around from room to room.

One older doctor yelled into the phone. "Can't they deliver it faster?! We don't have time! These people are going to die!" He slammed the phone and ran back down the hall.

Dr. Keen soon came back looking hurried. "I'm sorry for that. I need you to leave. I can not discuss your husband right now. There was some sort of bus accident. There are so many injuries. They need me now. Please come back tomorrow." He turned back around to dash out of the door.

"Cut it." Sarah spoke softly.

"Excuse me?" The doctor turned around and looked at her.

"Cut the plug. It's done." She smiled through her tears. "It's okay. It's going to be okay." She nodded softly.

"Mother!" Josh looked at her in shock. "What are you talking about?!" His expression slowly softened as he backed up and leaned against the wall, tears going down his face.

Dr. Keen called over some nurses who quickly pushed Alex's bed out as Sarah gave him one last kiss on the forehead. "It's okay baby." She whispered through her tears.

Dr. Keen walked over to Josh who was now sitting down with his face in his hands. "Your parents have done a great thing." He smiled. "Be brave like them." Josh looked up at him. "8: 45 AM. Don't forget that. That's when your father saved a lot of lives." With that he left the room and closed the door.

The Years Later

"Congratulation. You have a beautiful and healthy little girl." A man in a white coat walked over to Josh. "Your wife is doing just fine as well. You can go in and see her in a bit."

"Thank you." Josh smiled big as he looked over at his mother and sister who were sitting in the chairs and smiling back. "You're a grandma!" He laughed and looked back at the doctor. "Miracle of birth. It's amazing huh?"

"Certainly is." The doctor nodded. "I get to see delivering babies everyday but still life is an amazing thing to me every time I see it being born."

"It's sad that sometimes people just don't appreciate it, you know?"

"Very true. You know I almost died a while back. It really makes you love life."

"Oh really?" Josh asked. "So what happened? Why are you still here?"

"Well." The doctor put his glasses in his coat pocket. "I had just started college. I was running late but I made it to the bus on time. Sometimes I wish I hadn't. The bus driver was drunk at 8 in the morning. Crazy guy I think. He crashed the bus. I remember the bus flipped so many times. I was brought to this hospital! Funny I ended up working here myself. I lost a lot of blood that day too. My heart was fried. I think I was really lucky. There was a man there. He was in an accident a couple of nights before I ended up there. He was alive but just a hollow shell really. His family decided it was time to let him go." He touched his chest. "This heart right here came from him. Now every night before I go to sleep I thank that man for saving my life."

TODAY IS MY LAST DAY

The Last Day

Sometimes it seems that you can't do something when you really want to do it. When someone tells you: you can't do this or you can't do that, this is when you go and try to do the said undoable thing. It can be for so many reasons. Maybe you are doing it to rebel against someone. Perhaps you are doing it to prove someone is wrong and show him or her you can be what he or she thought you could never be.

For Marcus this was something even he couldn't figure out. It all came upon him through an accident. When he was barely thirteen years year old, he had gone through his teenage angst and depression stage. He yelled at his parents and rushed up the stairs the night he turned 13. He went to his room and locked himself in there for two hours before making the decision to end his own life. The clock on his wall read 9:45 PM. He took a knife he had taken up to his room a day before to cut a sandwich and took it to his own neck. His first thought was regret. The pain was so tremendous that he had wanted to go back in time and kill himself for doing such a thing. He could remember he had fallen over on the ground as the blood from his neck dripped down. It all seemed to be in slow motion. As he laid down on the ground he could see a drop of blood catching up with him. The last thought he had at the moment was not the typical "your life flashing before your eyes" moment. He had thought to himself why did he reach the ground before that drop?

Then he opened his eyes. He didn't move an inch. He only looked at the clock on the wall through the corner of his eyes, 9:40. He quickly sat up at that moment and grabbed his neck. As he examined himself in the mirror he saw nothing wrong. The knife was placed on his computer desk where it had been at 9:45. He didn't understand what had happened. Maybe he had passed out. He glanced back at the carpet to be assured of what he thought. It didn't happen. The last drop of blood he had seen was on the carpet, the only thing remaining from this thing that had just happened to him.

"Marc?" His mother voice called out to him behind the door "Honey. Open up. Come down and have some ice-cream, okay?"

This was the first time it had happened to him. Then it was a week after. He never forgot about what happened. He still wondered what had gone down that night. This time he wanted to test it out. He wasn't mad at anyone. He didn't want to die. His body spoke to him telling him not to do it, yet his brain argued it, something says you shouldn't, then you should. He took a bottle of pills out of his mother's cabinet. He didn't read the bottle. Pouring the pills out, he took one deep breath. He took another one as he raised his hands up. He could see them shaken yet they didn't stop. He placed the pills in handfuls at a time chewing and swallowing. Marc sat down on the floor and leaned against the bathtub. The bathroom door was locked. He looked at his Spiderman watch, which read 8:30 AM. It was a Saturday morning. He didn't have any school to worry about.

It was only 10 minuets later when he started feeling a little dizzy. Twenty minutes passed and he could feel the contents of his stomach coming back up. He let it do so into the toilet. Then he felt a little better. Oddly enough his body said this was wrong. He opened the cabinets under the sink and took out a white bottle labeled bleach. Without any second thought he opened the bottle and emptied more than half of it contents into his stomach. This was it. It felt as though his insides were burning. He was in so much pain he started to cry. Just like that night he fell over onto the ground. This time it was much colder. The floor wasn't soft either as it had been. The impact seemed so much harder to him. He could feel the pain through his whole body. The taste in his mouth was so horrid. He wanted to scream for help but no sound came out. Then he caught a sight of the time. This time it had taken him half an hour to die. One thing remained the same. He opened his eyes again. This time he suddenly stood up and opened the cabinets. Under the sink the bleach was once again placed neatly. The bottle was full to the top. He was still alive and well.

Over the next 5 years he had tried ways imaginable to kill himself in the privacy of his room. He had felt so much pain one would think he would no longer feel it. He still did. He still felt the fear every time he did this. Every time he had gotten up like nothing ever happened. The clock had gone back in time to the time before he had done anything to himself. Then it was time for him to try it in public. He went down to the subway and waited till the last second for the subway train to come by. He ran and dashed himself towards the roaring train. He felt the pain for only a split second before opening his eyes and being back at the subway station. He stood there for 10 seconds in amazement. No one was looking at him. No one seems to know something had happened. Then he saw the train coming by and passing him like nothing had happened.

He tried this once again, this time on a building. He made sure he had gotten attention. People and camera crew were around him with all cameras pointed up at him. There were people all around. Then he jumped. Like the train the pain only lasted a split second. Then he looked down. He saw his computer desk. There was a clean piece of paper in front of him and a pencil in his hand. This was the piece of paper he had written his extravagant jumping suicide on. He started to move his hand again. He switched it all around. There was a different building. The suicide was an hour later. Once again it all went according to the plan yet his eyes opened back up to have him see where he had been at 7:00 PM. He was again at the computer desk with the clean paper.

The Now Day

Marcus was now 24 years old. He had just met a girl in college, this year. He was a senior in biochemistry major. The girl, Jane, was a smart girl at his same age yet finishing the last year of her medical school. She was already doing her internship in a local hospital. They had moved in together the month before. Marcus had it all hidden from her. Every night before they went to bed he would go to take his shower. He would wash his hair and body. Like any normal person he would step out of the shower and brush his teeth. A few seconds later he would kill himself. Still the pain was there and still he woke to the scene before it all happened. He would then go on about his day and get ready for bed. Nothing exciting had happened. He wasn't even sure why he kept doing this.

"Bye baby." She would say goodbye to him at night to go to work at the hospital till 12 midnight. She left after dinner and came back after midnight everyday. He would go to his last class and be back home around 9. Then he would do some work and a bit of studying and watch some TV.

"I have to stay a little late tonight. I'm sorry! I will be back home before 2 tonight, all right?" Jane had called him on October 14.

"Of course, take care. I have to stay up late to finish a paper anyway so it will be all fine here. If I'm asleep feel free to knock me over the head." They had shared a small chuckle before saying goodbye.

Marcus worked on his paper. He finished it at 11. There was some leftover rice and chicken in the fridge. He grabbed it and flipped through the channels. He stopped on some show on food in Thailand. He loved traveling. His family would always go somewhere new for vacation. It had become a hobby of his to see how many countries he could kill himself in. So far he had 10 on the list. Thailand was one of them. He loved it so much he even minored in the language. He always wanted to go back. Jane had joined him when he had gone. She had a mindset to go back one day and volunteer at some hospitals to help out after she had met a few kids staying at the hospitals there. Perhaps they would move there one day.

It was now past midnight, 12:13. He decided it was time for his shower. This time he chose the simple knife to throat trick he had used his first time. His watch read 12: 31.

He sat on the couch and dried his hair afterwards. Sarah came home at 2: 15.

"Marcus. Give me some water and sit down! You have to hear this!"

"What happened?" He handed her a glass of water and joined her on the couch.

"I now know this is what I always wanted to do. It was amazing?"

"Well what was? I want some excitement."

"There was this woman there. She just gave birth and there were some kind of complications. I was in the room with the doctor. It was amazing. She was almost dead. No. No. In fact she WAS dead. For a few seconds anyways." She spoke so fast he had to stop her for a moment and get her some more water to calm her down.

"It was so scary but at the same time so amazing. 12: 31 is not officially my lucky time of the day. I was helping out, Marc! I was giving her some shocks when she died. I didn't know what to do. But I waited a minute and than I did it again! She was dead and then she was alive."

"12 what?"

"What? Why does that matter now?" She shook her head and hugged him. "I want to save more lives like this."

He stood up and smiled. "You did great." He pointed to the shower. "Go take a warm shower and wind down now. You deserve it Miss Hero!" She kissed him and walked towards the bathroom.

"Hey. 12: 31 right?"

"Hmm? Oh yeah. I'm going to make it my lucky time of the day. Silly but . . ." She smiled and closed the shower door.

He hurried to his room and look at his "kill time" book. It was a notebook he started keeping 7 year ago. This was the 3rd book. He would write down the time he had killed himself and the time he had woken up at. Today's read: Dead at 12: 31. Awake at 12: 29.

He closed the book and sat down on the bed looking up at the ceiling and back down with a loud sigh of relief. "Getting somewhere after so many damn years. What am I?"

He walked to the window and opened it. "Huh god?" He smiled at himself and walked back to the bed.

Your Day

The next day he skipped his night class and went to the hospital at 7.

Jane was working on some papers. He didn't go there to see her. This wasn't his reason for visiting the place. He sat behind a wall out of her sight and waited. The moment finally came. An accident victim was rushed into the hospital. It was an older man. He was taken to the ER. He could hear them yelling about the critical condition of the man. This man was dying. Marcus quickly ran into the bathroom and closed the door in a stall. He took his pocket knife out and slashed his own neck. The minute he woke up he ran out toward the front desk.

"I'm sorry. A man was just taken here. He was my uncle. Please tell me what's going on?" He lied to the woman.

"One moment sir. The doctor is coming out now."

A few minutes later the doctor walked out. Marcus ran up to him using his acting skills to conjure up some tears. "Is he all right?"

"I'm sorry. We did all we could." The doctor gave him a sad smile and walked away.

"I see . . ." He sighed and walked away from the desk. "So much for that huh?" He sat there for a few more minuets before deciding to get up and leave. Before he left he saw a couple walking out of a room followed by a doctor. "It's really amazing. We thought we had lost him. But don't worry. He is stable now. Your son was very lucky."

"I'm sorry." Marcus walked up to them. "What was your son here for?"

"Excuse me?" The husband looked at him oddly.

"I mean. Well. Is he all right now?"

"Yes. Sorry sir do we know you?"

"Oh no. I just thought he . . . Um. The doctor said your son was dead?" He looked over at the doctor.

"Oh yes. It's interesting really. Some people can die for seconds. Even minutes and then be brought back to life. Honestly I don't even know what happened this time. We didn't do anything. The kid was dead and then he was alive."

"God was looking out for my child." The mother smiled with tears in her eyes.

"Yeah . . . God." Marcus nodded and left the couple with congratulations.

As he walked towards the door he was stopped by a nurse. "Dear. I'm sorry but you looked troubled. You know there is a mini chapel here in the hospital." She pointed the way. "Do go. It will help take whatever burden you have off of you."

Marcus sat on a chair in front of a giant cross as he spoke.

"So I kill myself and some lucky bastard gets my life? Is that how it works? Is that really fair? Huh Almighty Lord?" He sighed and rubbed his eyes. Then he stopped his thinking and stared at the cross for a moment. He nodded slowly as he let a breath out. With a smile on his face he rubbed his hand together as if he was warming them up. "I guess it is." He nodded, as his smile got bigger. "A life for a life. It's still a life. I guess I can't complain."

A STRANGER'S SMILE

This was like any other day for David Wheeler, until it happened.

David woke up at 7 like every other morning and got ready for work. He was a 29-year-old man working in a men's suit shop. Valentino, Gucci, Hugo Boss, Dolce&Gabbana, Boggi Milano, Divacci, Dior, Ralph Lauren; they sold it all. He himself wore a suit to work everyday. A black Gucci suit always paired with black pants, a white shirt, and some sort of slanted striped tie. Today he chose a dark blue and black combination.

He grabbed some coffee on the way to work. The store was located in a huge shopping mall in New York, always crowded with hundreds of people. They had good business there and sold at least 10 suits worth $300 or more a day. He liked his job. It was a simple job and he was a simple man. He had a simple look with black hair neatly combed, black eyes, and a very light tan skin tone. His built was average with no bulging fat anywhere.

He was never one to go for any adventure. He always followed the pack and never strayed from what was known as normal. He didn't like to get too much attention and always blended himself with the environment around him.

He would take the subway and then walked about 10 minuets to get to work. His car engine needed a checkup for about a week now but he saw no point in fixing it. He liked the walk. He paid for his coffee and walked out of the store to start his walk. The streets were crowded with people of all kinds. He waited at a light with many others. He just drank his coffee and made no effort to look around. The light turned green after 20 seconds. David was reading the paper as he started walking with the crowd.

He was suddenly knocked off his feet and pushed forward. Everything went dark for a moment before he finally noticed what had happened. He was on the ground.

"Hey! You should really pay attention when you are crossing the street." The man who had pushed him out of the way of a car was looking down at him. His coffee was spilt on the ground and was now all over his paper.

"Oh my god!" David stood up and wiped himself off. "Thank you." He stared at the man still a little in shock.

"No problem. Just don't read and walk again." The man patted him on the shoulder before walking away. Everyone around him was staring now. Some people with a shocked look on their faces and others were whispering to one another.

"I'm . . . All right." He picked up his coffee-drenched paper and fast walked past everyone and around the corner as their eyes followed him.

David stood against the wall and rubbed his eyes breathing a bit too fast to be normal. He shook his head and took a deep breath in and out before continuing his walk to work.

As he arrived at work he walked straight to the back. His coworker was in the process of checking all the manikins before opening the store. The tall African American man, himself was dressed just as neat and well as the manikins. His nametag read Marcus. "Hey Dave!" He said as David walked past him. He raised his hand to acknowledge him and continued walking. He went to the back and closed the door behind himself. The room was filled with many boxes of hangers, bubble wrap, and many other closed boxes, which David knew was their merchandise. He slid down on the floor and robbed his eyes. There was an odd throbbing pain that seemed to be coming from his brain and going to the back of his eyes. "Ah . . ." He closed his eyes tightly which caused him to scrunch his face.

"Opening." Markus called from the other side of the door. He knocked on the door a few times. "You okay?"

"Yeah. Yeah I'm fine." David stood up and shook his head. He fixed his jacket and examined himself in the little mirror on the wall. "Open." He said to Marcus as he walked out of the back room.

He took his place in front of the door as he always did. There was another man working there. He was older than the two but in better shape than both of them. He looked like he should be modeling the suits not selling them. "Good morning." He said to David.

David nodded and smiled. "Morning John."

A group of ladies walked in 30 minutes after the store had opened. "Can I help you with anything today?" David smiled at them. They seemed to be in their mid thirties and dressed well enough to be able afford a $400 suit easily.

"I'm looking for something for my husband's birthday." The lady in the front answered. "Something dark navy blue. Nothing too flashy, just something he could wear to official meetings."

"I think I have the best thing for you then. Follow me ladies." He led them to a Mishumo blue navy suit in the farther back of the store. "This should be perfect." He took one off the rack and handed it to her to examine. As he pulled his hands out from under the suit his hand grazed hers. He pulled back suddenly yanking the jacket to the floor. He stared at her feeling a bit shocked.

"Are you all right?" She asked as her friends stared at David like he was an alien.

"Oh yes. I'm sorry. I will get you another one." He turned around and reached up for another suit.

The lady reached for his hand to stop him before he got another one. "Could you get me a large size?" She said.

David didn't feel right. As the woman's hand touched his it was like his mind went blank. It was like a movie playing in his eyeballs. He could hear the cry of a baby. Everything was dark and suddenly there was a little blue blanket and then there was a little wooden crib. He didn't feel like he was physically there. The black started melting away as a bedroom appeared. It was a like a nursery. Suddenly he was at the crib looking down at the baby. His fear started to fade as he looked at the laughing baby's face. As he looked up he saw two people standing next to him. The woman he had heard before all this was one of them. Next to her was a man a little bit on the chubby side. They both looked so happy with joyful smiles gracing their faces. The woman reached down and grabbed the baby's small hands.

"Sir?" He was suddenly snapped out of it. He let out a gasp for air and turned around to look at the scared ladies behind him. "Are you all right?" The woman from his vision looked at him concerned.

"What happened?" David asked, looking around nervously.

"I grabbed your hand when I told you to get me a large size. My husband is a bit on the chubbier side you see." She started to trail off the subject for a bit. "Anyways you just froze suddenly."

"I'm sorry. It's-"

"Just one of those days?" the woman cut him off. Her friends had walked away to go look at other things now. "Don't worry about it. I've been having those days a lot too lately. Feeling so sick and . . ." The expression on her face was sorrowful. ". . . I and the husband have not been doing too well." She sighed and looked at a coat next to her on a rack. "It seems like something is missing. You know what I mean?" She looked up at him.

He nodded still confused about what he had seen. In his mind he had a sudden flashback to the scenes in his head. He saw the baby's smiling face as he looked at the woman.

"I'm sorry. I'm telling you my life's story and I'm here supposed to be shopping." She shook her head. "I'll take the one you showed me, but a large one."

David grabbed a large size of the coat and walked with her to the cash register. "He will wrap and ring it up for you." He handed the suit to her. Before he let go he looked up at her and said. "I'm sure things will work out. You'll find that missing piece soon." He smiled and walked away toward the front door. The woman watched him walking away; smiling.

David stood there staring at the door. The woman smiled at him as she walked out with her purchase.

Marcus walked up next to him. "Hey man you sure you are okay?"

David was now rubbing his eyes again. "Yeah, just a little headache."

"Go home. Today is a slow day. I'll cover for you." He patted him on the back.

On any other sickness he would have refused but today he just didn't feel right. He nodded. "Thanks," and walked out as he took his nametag off. He stopped by a coffee place and looked at the coffee choices. He took off his coat and rolled up his jacket's sleeves to avoid getting too hot. Finally he made his choice and waited on the side for his drink.

A young man maybe 18 years old walked past him heading to the bathroom and accidentally bumped into him. The boy's arm hit David's and then it happened again. Everything went black. And then he saw him. The boy was standing in the middle of the darkness with a phone in his hand. He could hear a voice from the emptiness. "We found a donor for your mother."

Then it was all back to normal. The boy was next to him grabbing his two cups of coffee. "Is this one yours?" He pointed to the cup sitting next to his.

David picked it up, his hand shaking a bit. What was happening to him?

From the boy's pocket came a typical phone ring tone. "Oh sh*t!" The boy almost dropped his coffee trying to get his phone. He put one of the drinks down. David wanted to move but he was still in that odd shock.

"Hello?" The boy answered his phone. David turned his head and looked at him. The boy slowly put the other coffee down on the counter. "What!?" He looked shocked. Then a smile appeared on his face and his eyes started to water. "Thank you." He hung up the phone and let his hand drop to his side. The boy looked like he was trying to hold his tears back. His smile got bigger and he dashed out of the store leaving his coffees.

"What was that about?" The man making a blended coffee drink behind the counter asked as he looked at David. "Weird kid, man!"

"I think . . ." David looked down at his coffee. He walked out of the store without saying another word.

David chugged his iced coffee. He ran out of the shopping center and looked around. He ran up to a girl standing there alone and grabbed her hand.

This time it wasn't just darkness. It was a chapel with lots of people. It was a beautiful wedding. The girl was at the entrance walking down with a much older gentleman; perhaps her father. She was shining in a white wedding dress. A young boy was standing at the alter in his suit. He smiled at her as she walked down the aisle.

"Hey!" She yanked her hand away and pushed David to the ground. "You freak!" He looked up at her as the boy from his vision grabbed her hand. "Let's go. Damn freak . . ." They walked away from him. David smiled at them and whispered "Congratulations" as he stood up and slowly walked toward the subway.

*   *   *

A month passed since that day and by now David knew what it all was. A single touch from someone was all it needed to be triggered. He could see into their mind, into their future. What he saw was the happiest day for them to come. It was like a happy movie playing in his head. He had seen many lives, many beautiful moments. He had seen a little girl's father returning from Iraq. He had seen a young doctor saving a dying man's life. He had seen beautiful weddings and amazing reunions. The only price for this was the headaches and the eye pain. To him it was worth it. It had given him happiness. It was like living in a never-ending feel-good movie.

He stood at the door in his suit with a smile on his face as always.

"Hey." Marcus came up behind him.

"Hey. How is your mother?"

"What? I didn't think I told you about the surgery." He looked at David. "Well, I guess I did, huh?" He smiled and continued. "It went perfect. She is doing much better now. I feel like . . . It was a miracle; the best day of my life." He rubbed his eyes trying not to lose this tough guy attitude by shedding any tears. "Oh hello!" He greeted a customer and followed her to help.

David smiled and laughed a bit. "Welcome." A young woman came in. "How may I help you?"

"I'm looking for a suit for my father. My wedding is in 3 months and I wanted to buy him a suit now. He is . . . going on a trip soon and I want to buy this just in case he doesn't have time when he comes back . . . If he makes it." Her voice got quieter as the last part left her lips.

"Excuse me?" David couldn't really hear her last sentence.

"Nothing, nothing! So that suit?"

"Oh yes. Well for wedding. A simple one is always good." He walked with her. His eyes were hurting again but by now he was just used to it. He moved his hand over a bit to touch hers only for a second. He wanted to get a glimpse into her happiness. He was in a chapel as he had been many times before. This time he was behind the main door, however. The girl was standing there in her dress. She was staring at the door with tears in her eyes as her mom comforted her. Then the door opened and an elderly man in a black tux walked in. She ran to him and hugged him tightly. David smiled as the vision ended. The image slowly faded like always but this time he didn't see the store. He didn't see the girl.

"Sir? Are you all right?" The girl spoke to him. He could hear the sounds of the store and the mall. He could hear Marcus talking to a customer, but all he could see was darkness, just a black wall. He moved his hand in front of his face and still nothing. He touched his own face and could feel it all, but he saw nothing.

He wasn't freaked out. He didn't panic. Somehow in his head he always knew this would come. He smiled and asked the girl. "If you could only see everyone else's happiness but never see any of your own, how do you think your life would be?"

"Huh? I guess pretty boring?" She replied.

He continued smiling and said "You always see yourself smiling in the mirror and it's so repetitive. Your smile doesn't cheer you up. You never think if other people are smiling too. But when a stranger is feeling so much pain and you smile at them; that smile gives them so much love. When you see a stranger's smile, when you see a stranger's happiness; isn't that worth a million times more than seeing your own?"

DUST UNDER MY FEET

The Start of the Road

The ground then felt so soft under my feet. It felt like I was walking on sand yet my feet did not sink into it. I kept rubbing my eyes as I looked around. *This feels so real but it can't be. Can this be real?*

"Hello?" I yelled as I finally built up enough strength and courage to look at this odd ground. It was white and soft. It was more like ash than sand. "Please someone answer me!" I kept yelling but no one seemed to be around.

I looked around and saw nothing for miles and miles and miles. My brain was still fuzzy. I stopped rubbing my eyes and slowly came back to my senses. *Where was I last?* Closing my eyes, I thought back to before this all happened.

Step into Your Life

I was sitting in my cubicle. It was a tiny one. The kind you don't want to end up in, but do anyways due to your job at a huge law firm where only the almighty select few get their own office. Along with that they get the big house, the expensive cars, and the hot wives, all of which I did not own. I live in a one bedroom apartment next to a crazy old lady who collects dead stuffed birds. Of course she is a sweet lady who never fails to bring me some of the "lovely" pastries she makes. They taste like crap. Nevertheless, it's the thought that counts, right?

It's not a bad life, but I wouldn't mind a hot wife who also cooks delicious foods for me or a nice cozy car to drive to work instead of my old beat up black beauty. I call her f**king piece of sh*t that never works. It's a fitting name.

My job isn't much of an exciting one either. I might be a lawyer but the best court action I've ever got was when I was defending some guy who got charged for kicking some other guy's car. Someone actually splashed the judge with water. I know; it's so very exciting!

At the same time I guess my life isn't that bad. At least I have my looks. I never was the kind to be a narcissist but I have to admit I look good. I'm a little too pale and skinny but I think my blue eyes and black hair make up for it. Although I shouldn't be saying that since I haven't had a relationship for three years now. My last one ended when I was 27 years old. I'm not sad about it anymore.

What did I do that day? I finished work and drove home. My car broke down on the way home, again. I had it towed home and passed out on my couch for a long time. I woke up to this, whatever this is. It is night time but I can still see fairly well. For some reason the moon seems closer and brighter. It even looks bigger now.

I put up my hand towards the moon to measure it. It's the size of a basketball. Now I know something is not right. Although the lack of my apartment building and every other building around was a bigger hint.

"Hello?" I said again as I started walking. It was cold. It has never been this cold during spring here. My suit was still on me. I didn't change out of it before I laid down the day before. I was missing my tie. I think I took it off. My memory was still a little hazy. "What is going on?" I spoke to myself.

Step by Step

I had now walked for at least an hour. Still nothing was in sight. Other people would probably be freaked out by now but I never did. I could cut off my finger and still calmly dial 911. I could imagine that conversation, "Oh yes hello. It seems that I have managed to cut off my finger here. Could you kindly send some sort of fixer upper man here to fix this?" I chuckled to myself as I imagined it all in my head.

"Hey!" I heard someone says. As I looked a bit more carefully and my mind cleared up I could see what looked like the 7-Eleven store I used to visit late in the night before I had learned to cook for myself. This however looked like something out of an apocalyptic movie. The store roof was half ripped off and the inside looked as though it had been pummeled by a pack of very hungry people. Thankfully most of the food was still there; I was starting to get hungry. Some water sounded good too. This air was so dry.

"Hey you man!" I started walking towards the man calling me. He was standing in front of the now crooked door with what looked like a Snickers bar in one hand and a can of Red Bull in the other.

"What happened?" I asked him. "Where is everything?"

He looked at me. "Why you askin' me?" He was a tall man. Not taller than me though. Looking at the fact that I'm 6'4" you can see why not many people are taller than me. His hair was sleek, straight and long. He had pulled it back into a loose low ponytail. From what I could see he was probably Hawaiian. "The store was dead empty man. So I closed up and took a nap. I woke up to this. Crazy sh**t man, right?" He took a big bite out of his Snickers bar and finished the rest of his Red Bull all in one gulp. "I knew I shouldn't have come to work. F**king messed up my best shirt too." He was wearing a black undershirt with a white bottom up shirt over it. I only guessed it was white since it had been ripped and torn and now was covered in gray dust and dirt.

"You work here?" I asked. He must have been a high school dropout. He looked to be in his early twenties.

"Worked you mean?"

"Yea . . . I guess it's worked now."

I pushed the door open and walked in. Most of the food boxes were on the floor now. I grabbed a Twix bar from the ground and walked to the fridge which was no longer functioning, not were any of the lights in the store. He had been smart and had put up some candles around the place. Not as dumb as he looked I guess.

"Ey man. You gotta pay for that." He said as I grabbed a water bottle out of the fridge. He was now in the store by what used to be the cash register. It looked more like a lump of broken down metal now.

I looked at him with a shocked "you have got to be kidding me" look on my face.

"Ha Man! Just sh**tin' ya." He said as he laughed his ass off at a joke that wasn't even funny. "I guess money ain't gonna matter here anymore." He finally said after his laughter subsided. "What's your name?"

"Daniel Ryden." I replied to him as I ate my Twix.

"Kei Nihipali" He reached his hand out for me to shake.

I placed my water bottle of an empty shelf and shook his hand. "Nihipali? Never heard that one before. Hawaiian?" I wanted to check myself.

"Half. Mom is Japanese." I was close.

"I don't know what's going on here but I feel like we need to go see if there is anyone else alive." I suggested. "You got a bag around here?"

"Yeah." Kei walked to the back room and brought out a backpack. He opened it and emptied out all its contents. I examined them. This is where the saying "don't judge a book by its cover" popped into my head. "You're a med student?" I asked.

"Yeah." He cleaned up his mess of papers and went behind the cash register. "Here," He threw the bag at me.

"Thanks." I caught the bag and started stuffing some pre-made sandwiches they had in the store into it: Ham, Turkey, Roast Beef. I left the tuna. It would be the first one to go bad.

"Fuel for the road?" He asked. I nodded in reply. Kei was organizing his papers and placing them in the storage department under the counter. "Grab some Doritos." He told me. "My fave." he said as he walked to the fridges and grabbed some water bottles.

I grabbed a few bags of Doritos and other chips and stuffed them into the bag. "Not enough room in here" I said as I tried to force two water bottles in.

"Sides."

"Oh." I placed them in the side water bottle holders. "Let's go."

We walked out. As I walked away I saw him stopping to lock the door. "What's the point?" I asked.

"My school text books; My notes are in there too." He said as he caught up with me. There was something about this attitude and dedication he had that made me admire him and give him more respect than I did when I first met him. I needed to respect him. I knew he might be the only friend I would have from now on.

Take New Steps

We had walked for so long now. All around us we had seen buildings that were half demolished or more. So many buildings were full gone with nothing left; not even the people. Every once in a while we would run into some stray cats or dogs.

"Why isn't the sun up yet?" Kei asked as he glanced at the oversized moon. "I think we been walking on and off for more than . . ." He glanced at his wristwatch. "Stupid thing." He tapped it with his finger a few times before taking it off and throwing it on the ground. "Technology is broke; It's night forever; and there are no people or buildings around."

I sat down on what remained of the back of a truck. The front of the car was almost all gone which left a slanted back. "I guess it's some kind of apocalypse."

"Then why are we alive?"

"Haven't figured it out yet." I pulled out a turkey sandwich and gave half of it to Kei. "I guess we will find out soon enough."

"Hey! Is that food?" The voice was a woman's and came from what seemed far away. It was starting to get foggy and hard to see now.

"Hey. Over here." She called out again.

"Dan! Dan!" Kei hit my arm. "Someone else!" Kei walked towards the voice. "Hey. Come here. Lady!"

The woman finally appeared out of the fog and next to Kei. She was a tall woman, maybe six feet tall. Her hair was a light brown color with light waves and her eyes were a bright green color. Her skin was flawless with a nice subtle tan color.

"It is food." I stood up and walked to her with a turkey sandwich.

"Thank you. I haven't eaten since, well, since I woke up to this."

"Woke up?" I asked as I watched her devouring the sandwich. Though she wasn't very clean I had to admit she was beautiful.

"Well there is the key to why we are alive." Kei said.

"What?" She had finished her sandwich and was eyeing the water bottle in the bag.

"Here." I handed it to her. "Me and him were both sleep when it happened and we are now alive."

"I see." She smiled. "Thanks for the food and water." She said. "My name is Melina."

"I'm Daniel, This is Kei." By now I knew much more about Kei due to our walking conversations. It was time to get to know her.

Step Forward

It has now been two years. We still don't know what happened that day but we do know we are not the only ones alive. We have found others, people who traveled days, weeks, and even months before they got to us. We spent four months to built this shelter where we are living now. We worked everyday.

It's a nice place; right under the 7-Eleven where Kei had worked. There was a big storage room. We worked hard and made it even bigger. In fact it is now big enough for us and all the others who have joined us to live comfortably. All fifty three people live here now. It wasn't as hard as you think. It was me, Kei, and Mel. We worked for two month alone then one day a group showed up at the 7-Eleven.

Mel brought up the great idea to put up a sign on the door, which read: SURVIVORS HERE. We used a can of paint from the storage room to write it.

The group itself had been only two people strong when it started and along the way had flourished into ten people. Then another group showed up two months after. Seven more people showed up the next month. In the next three months we had gotten a few others. The last group was four Japanese people, a brother and his sister along with two others. They showed up about three months ago and by now had made themselves part of our huge family. This had made our family fifty two people strong. Six months later Mel and I welcomed our first child. His name is Kyle.

We sent groups out every week to go find food. The supplies have been neatly organized thanks to Mel and a couple of other ladies. Among us are four engineers, and five teachers. We have a chef and many others that can cook. Kei has now become one of our doctors along with one of the Japanese men named Jin who had joined us. Before all this, Jin had been a family doctor. With this we have managed to build ourselves a new civilization from the ground up.

Things are looking up for us all.

Take One Step Back

Kyle is almost seven years old now. He has his mother's beautiful green eyes and my pale skin and black hair. He is quite an energetic child.

These days I'm looking back on what my wife had said to me only a few years back. Her voice is always in my head. "Never worry about the future. As long as you keep what you love by your side, you will have a rich future, baby." Her voice was so sweet. I wish I could hear it again. I wish she were still by my side.

During the time when food was low, diseases had manifested themselves. Kei and Jin did all they could to help save people. They managed to save three people from the new disease, which no one had even seen before this time. Mel had been working so hard. She helped clean everything. She took care of Kyle and two other kids who had been orphaned. She took care of the elderly and helped cook. She never let on to it. I didn't know. If I knew I would do all I could. I never wanted to loose her. Jin and Kei lost ten people. One of them was Melina Ryden.

Things were not as I thought they would be. We ran out of food two years ago. Many of the people that had been with us had left. They wanted to survive. Our new family was not as strong as it seemed. Now only a few remained. We, ten people were closer than ever. We did not live in the comfort of our shelter anymore. We had not seen sunshine in nine years. We had barely eaten for the past month. We wore the same cloths for so long and only had water when we reached a river. Everywhere was like a dusty dead desert. The water was dirty most of the time. No one cared. We drank it and we washed in it. If we were lucky we would catch a fish or two. We were always traveling. We needed to, if we wanted to survive. The weather never changed. It never rained. It was never hot. We were lucky that it was never too cold. We put the two kids we had ahead of ourselves, always. Food and water were always first for them. One was Kyle and the other was Kei's daughter who had been born a year after him. She took after her father with her smartness and after her mother with her silk smooth black Japanese hair and pale skin.

Kei had fallen for Jin's sister and the two married only a month after they met. In such a small world it was easy for you to find your love. They named their baby Kimiko after his wife's mother. She was a beautiful girl. She and Kyle were the best of friends. With them being the only two kids they had grown attached and refused to be separated.

We had been moving for almost a year now. It was a hard year. How hard? We had started this with twenty people.

Take the Last Step

It's been twenty-two years now since the day everything changed. I'm a lot skinnier now. My black hair is grey. I miss it sometimes. I used to hate that cubicle. I used to hate that car. I used to hate the old lady's cookies. Now it's all I want. I would kill for another taste of her cookies. I would kill for another moment in that cubicle. I would kill to sit at my desk and handle the most boring case in the world. I never knew what people meant when they said don't take what you have for granted because when it's gone you will miss it. I never thought I had much. I never thought anything I had was worth a single moment of joy in life. At this moment all I want is that back. All I want is to make it right and give it the moments of joy it deserved. I want to hold my wife's hand and watch my son playing in a playground. I miss the smell of grass. I miss people.

In the last thirteen years we have struggled but we lived. Jin is now dead and gone along with five more of everyone who was left. I myself have lost so much. I am much paler now. I haven't eaten in so long. Looking around I can see Kyle picking up some wood to make us a fire. I am proud of him. He looks much better then I did at his age. He has muscles which I never had but dreamed so much of getting. He has his brain from his mother. He has her smile. He has my voice.

I can See Kimiko cleaning the fish we managed to catch. Kei is sleep. He looks as bad as I do.

Even with all the dirt and her hair pulled back into a messy bun, even while cleaning a fish Kimoko looks beautiful. After all these years those two are still inseparable.

The ash is so soft under my body. I have grown to love this ash as a bed.

"Papa," Kimiko called me that. "Can I have the lighter from Dad's bag?" She smiled at me.

I grab Kei's bag and hand it to her. "Hey. Wake up." I shook him. He slowly opened his eyes and looked over at his daughter. "Is the food ready?" His voice was weak now. The old man's voice is much like mine. He had cut his hair short.

"Almost. Get up old man." Kimiko chuckled as she lit the wood my son had brought.

"I might be old but in my days I could beat you in basketball any day. I could beat Kyle over here too." Kei said as he used the rock he was leaning against to help him get up and made his way over to us.

"I'm sure you could; whatever this basketball is." Kimiko placed the fish on a stick and on the fire.

"Look what I found" Kyle pulled out a fake red rose. "Must have been a fake flower shop here before."

"How pretty!" Kimiko looked at it.

"For you." He leaned over and placed it in her bun.

Watching this scene I looked at Kei who had the same smile I had on, on his face.

Perhaps I couldn't go back in time to give my life the joy it deserved, but I now know what that joy feels like.

"Dad? Dad! Kei? Dad!"

"Papa! Papa! . . ."

That night everyone who had been alive when "It" happened died.

Create New Steps

"Daniel. Get back in the house now." I sat on the couch watching my wife Kimiko at the front door. "It's about to rain and you don't want to get sick right before your first day of school starts."

I could hear baby-crying coming from upstairs.

"Baby. Go check on your daughter." Kimiko smiled at me as she dried Dan up with a blue towel. He had run in only after the rain started pouring down.

"My daughter!? It takes two to make a baby."

"Well yes, and one is taking care of this one that the two made. Change a diaper once in a while dear. You *NEED* to get over your fear of poop." She kept smiling as she spoke to me.

I shook my head smiling back at her. "Yes Ma'am!" I got off the couch and went up the stairs. Mika was the newest addition to our family. She was only a couple of months old now. I closed the door to my 6-year-old son's room before going into Mika's and picking her up.

"Dinner!" I heard Daniel say.

"Don't yell!" Kimiko followed.

"But you just yelled mama!"

"Yes! You see how annoying it is?!" After a few moments of silence I could see and hear the two laughing as I went down the stairs with Mika.

The table was set and the food was on the table. "Smells like my favorite."

"Spaghetti with meatballs, vegetable soup, and some yummy yummy salad."

"Euw. Salad!" Daniel and I said in synch.

"You owe me a soda." I said as I sat Mika down on her booster seat.

"Papa can I have two dollars to buy you a soda?"

I smiled and picked him up. "I'll let it go this time if you promise to be good on your first day of school, Deal?"

He nodded his head and I placed him in his seat. I sat down next to him across from my wife. "God! We thank you for this dinner."

Take Slow Steps and Enjoy the Ride

I woke up to Daniel jumping on my back. "Dad! Wake up! You have to drive me to my first day of school." He was still in his PJs. Kimiko sat up next to me where she was sleeping.

"Go wash your face and I will come help you get dressed." she said.

Daniel ran out the room and into the bathroom with so much excitement that I was sure he would explode.

"Good morning baby." I sat up and kissed my wife on the lips.

"Good morning." She smiled and went into our bathroom to get ready for her day. She ran her own restaurant now. Perhaps her years on the road having to cook for so many people were the start of her future.

I got out of bed and walked to the balcony. That day when I lost my father was the day this started.

I opened the curtains and the bright sunlight beamed in. Then I opened the balcony door and stepped out. I let the cool fall breeze hit my face. I could see the city beaming with energy as people walked and drove to start their day.

"Your suit is on the table"

"Thank you." I walked back in. Kimiko was now helping Dan get dressed. I put on my suit and walked down the stairs to watch the news and grab some coffee. I always needed something to give me energy for my job. I'm a lawyer. I need my energy to survive in the fish tank of a law firm. I was one of the lucky ones I must say. I make the big money and live in a big mansion of a house. I own a hundred thousand dollar car too. The most important thing is that I have the most beautiful and amazing wife around. Even still I take joy in every moment because I know what it's like not to have this joy. Oh; and I have my own Office.

The End Is Just A Beginning